MIRROR

Alexandra Day & Christina Darling

Farrar · Straus · Giroux New York

For Chris and Randall

—C.D.

My thanks to Hillela, her dog, Sadie,
and her mother, Laura, for their enthusiastic and patient modeling.
Thanks also to Virginia Stratton, Patten Wilson, Rose O'Neill,
and Charles Folkard

—A.D.

Published simultaneously in Canada by HarperCollins*CanadaLtd*
Library of Congress catalog card number: 96-84953
Color separations by Hong Kong Scanner Craft
Printed and bound in the United States of America by Berryville Graphics
First edition, 1997

I am writing this story because my fifth-grade teacher, Miss Riley, said that if I wanted to be a writer when I grow up, I should practice this summer, and because something happened to me that is very amazing.

Before I start, I want to say that I DO NOT TELL LIES (at least not about important things). If you don't believe me, you can ask my best friend, Rachel. So when I say that this is really true, you can trust me.

It all happened when I was seven. During the summer we helped my mother's best friend, Jeanette, move from an apartment into a house. She had a mirror that her great-uncle gave her that she was afraid the movers would break, so my mother hung it in my room. I guess she figured my room was the safest place in the house.

The real story began on the afternoon my mother forced me to take a nap. I don't know how many times I have told her that seven is much too old for a nap, but sometimes my mother has stubborn opinions. I was lying on my bed staring at my bookshelf and wondering if I would get in trouble if my mother caught me reading, when out of the corner of my eye I swear I saw a *real* jungle in Jeanette's mirror with tigers and snakes moving around and everything.

You can imagine how fast I got over to the mirror, but when I looked it was just a plain mirror again. I was almost positive I had seen something, but I stared at it for a long time and nothing happened.

I decided maybe I could fool it by pretending to read, but just as soon as I thought I saw something, I would turn quick to look at it and it would be blank.

I tried showing it a book that always makes me laugh (no matter how hard I try not to).

I tried looking out the window and being very interested in a squirrel outside. But however fast I looked back at the mirror, I could never see anything I was sure about.

Well, after dinner I was very excited about going to bed. (I am sure you would have been, too.) So I changed into my nightgown, brushed my teeth, and went to my room, saying I was going to play with my paper dolls (as you can see, that is a very small lie). This time I tried some new things to fool the mirror into being magical for me. I also tried some of the same things, but nothing worked. So finally, since I was only seven and still very immature, I got mad and said out loud, "Oh, you're just a plain old mirror after all!"

Boy,
was
I
wrong!

I guess it really wanted to show off.

It must have gotten later than I thought, because I was surprised when Mother yelled up, “Turn off that light right now!”

Over the next couple of days the mirror showed me that it did not only do things when we were alone.

Certain visitors noticed it, and others, lucky for me, did not. Sometimes I thought it was being very funny, but other times it was just plain rude.

The worst time was when my cousin Susan came to stay overnight. I have never really liked Susan because she is one of those kids who cry all the time and tell on you to grownups whenever they can. I was positive she would tell about the mirror if she saw it being magic. So before she came I covered the glass part with some sweaters and towels.

I noticed after we were put to bed that a
:orner was showing and the mirror
vas making angry pictures
ınd colors at me. I guess
t was mad at being
overed up.

So I
told Susan
that we had a very
bad flying-bug problem
in our house at night and
convinced her to sleep with her
head under the covers (leaving her
nose sticking out to breathe, of course).

I started thinking that maybe all mirrors were magical and I just hadn't noticed it before. I tried looking into as many as I could. But I never saw anything special.

Because it was summertime, my mother said I could stay up and read until nine every night. But what I really wanted to do was play with the mirror. It took me all kinds of places, but I never got to stay.

Well, finally the horrible day came that Jeanette was ready to have her mirror back. I was very sad when they took it from my room, but of course I didn't cry (though I know my mother thought I did and gave me her handkerchief).

That night when it was time to go to bed, my mother told me she had a surprise for me and she brought in a new mirror and hung it in the same place.

But without Jeanette's mirror my room seemed very quiet and empty, so I didn't play in there for a couple of weeks. But then I kind of forgot to think about it every day. As a matter of fact I hadn't thought about it for a long time before I decided to write this story.

But I guess I will always hope that I will meet a magic mirror again.